"Tolerance is respect, acceptance and appreciation of the rich diversity of our world's cultures, our forms of expression and ways of being human."

United Nations Educational, Scientific and Cultural Organization (UNESCO)

Millie Brown Sees Music
Written and Illustrated by Breayanna Robinson & Milena Tyler von Wrangel
Text and illustrations copyright © 2008 by B'nai B'rith International

Published as part of the *Diverse Minds Youth Writing Challenge* by:

B'NAI B'RITH INTERNATIONAL

2020 K Street NW, 7th Floor
Washington, DC 20006
202-857-6600
www.bnaibrith.org

Millie Brown sees Music

Written by:
Breayanna Robinson

Illustrated by:
Milena Tyler, von Wrangel

Millie Sees Music: by
Breayanna Robinson and
Milena Tyler von Wrangel for
B'nai B'rith Diverse Minds
Scolarship
March 18, 2008

Millie Brown has a frown
because she sees music upside down
backwards notes that flip around
broken tunes without a sound

Then Mrs Flows brings a book
So Millie Brown can take a look
of music heard from around the
world
and shed a little light on this
silly girl

Millie Brown scans the page
as music from . . .

Mrs. Flows says, "My music is so wonderful. Care to share with the lass tommorow, why music will always be coloorful?

Millie Brown begins to frown
Her mind flops upside down
Broken tunes without a sound.
Backwards notes flip around.

Scared to see how joyful music can be
Within its place and time and creativity
Mrs. Flows says, "Music can be free
because of diversity."

The next day in class, Millie Brown tells her friends
of all the joyous sounds and beats and music blends

They all hold hands, a circle of wonders
Reminding the world that music is simply colors.

B'nai B'rith International

Diverse Minds Youth Writing Challenge

Millie Brown Sees Music, written and illustrated by Breayanna Robinson and Milena Tyler von Wrangel, was created as part of the B'nai B'rith International *Diverse Minds Youth Writing Challenge* for Los Angeles County.

The *Diverse Minds Youth Writing Challenge* is an education and awareness initiative created by B'nai B'rith International as part of its series of programs developed to combat bigotry through the promotion of tolerance and equality. The contest aims to present positive views about diversity to a broad range of youth in order to achieve tolerance within our communities.

Executed through public and private high schools within several communities, the contest asks high school students to write and illustrate a children's book that tells a story of diversity and tolerance. Participants were required to think about how these principles can improve our world, and then create innovative ways to teach these ideas to children through the creation of a book.

Book submissions were reviewed by a local judging panel comprised of business leaders, educators, authors and religious officials. Scholarship prizes in the amounts of $5,000, $2,000 and $1,000 are awarded to the first, second and third place winners, and the first-place winning books are professionally published and distributed to elementary schools, libraries and youth organizations within each winner's community.

In the 2007-2008 school year, this innovative program was offered in Los Angeles, New York City, Colorado Springs, CO, Minneapolis/St. Paul, MN and the Washington, DC Metro area.

B'nai B'rith International would like to thank the Al and Stuart Herman Memorial Fund for their generous support of the Diverse Minds Youth Writing Challenge in Los Angeles County.

Millie Brown Sees Music

Written and Illustrated by

Breayanna Robins & Milena Tyler von Wrangel

Pacific Palisades Charter High School ✦ Los Angeles, CA

Teacher: Ms. Rose Gilbert

Breayanna Robins and Milena Tyler von Wrangel, seniors at Pacific Palisades Charter High School in Los Angeles, were selected as the first-place winners of the 2008 *Diverse Minds Youth Writing Challenge* in Los Angeles County. In addition to the publication and distribution of their book, they will split the $5,000 college scholarship prize.

Milena is an artist and Breayanna is a writer and they were pleased to combine their talents into the creation of this book, which they hope will broaden the minds of children around the world.

Second Place Winner

The Big Air

Written & Illustrated by

Crystal Lajeras Maranan

Third Place Winner

Driving Blind!

Written & Illustrated by

Samantha Wette & Melissa Wette

B'NAI B'RITH   INTERNATIONAL

B'nai B'rith International is the most widely known Jewish humanitarian, human rights, and advocacy organization. Since 1843, B'nai B'rith has been dedicated to improving the quality of life for those throughout the country and around the globe through programs that promote its commitment to youth, health education, senior housing, community service, public action and disaster relief. B'nai B'rith International's reach extends to more than 50 countries around the world.

Today, B'nai B'rith International is a national and global leader in helping communities in crisis; providing senior housing and advocacy on issues of vital concern to seniors and their families; and promoting diversity and tolerance education to our nation's youth.

The work of B'nai B'rith International is focused in its Centers: Senior Services, Community Action, and Human Rights & Public Policy. These Centers provide the framework for intensive study of issues and thoughtful responses through the combined efforts of dedicated volunteer leaders and professional staff. Please enjoy the following descriptions and photographs which highlight a sample of B'nai B'rith's many activities around the United States and across the world.

The Global Voice

From Sri Lanka to New Orleans to Darfur, B'nai B'rith seeks to fill the needs that might otherwise be overlooked. Whether it's helping to rebuild a community devastated by disaster or sponsoring a contest to develop children's books on diversity, B'nai B'rith reaches out to those hurt by intolerance and indifference, those whose lives have been disrupted by terrorism or natural tragedy; and the sick and the needy around the world.

Communities in Crisis
B'nai B'rith, in partnership with the Brothers Brother Foundation, has brought more than $64 million worth of medicines and supplies to Latin America, Cuba and Africa through the Communities in Crisis program.

Camp Passport
This program allows Israeli children between 10 and 16 who have been directly affected by terrorism to recapture a bit of their childhood by attending an all-expense paid B'nai B'rith summer camp experience.

Intercommunal Affairs
This Office develops partnerships with a diverse spectrum of faith-based and ethnic groups, and other key institutions, and advances the achievements by B'nai B'rith in the areas of civil rights, humanitarian aid and tolerance.

Office of United Nations Affairs
At the UN since its founding conference in San Francisco, B'nai B'rith International is the only Jewish non-governmental organization (NGO) with an office exclusively dedicated to United Nations affairs.

Disaster Relief
When disasters -natural and manmade- strike in the US or around the globe, B'nai B'rith raises funds and provides appropriate and ongoing help to those affected - and stay in the region when most others have moved on.

Enlighten America
This tolerance education program, designed for elementary and middle school ages, allows kids to create art projects that depict their ideas of diversity. The art project is coupled with a curriculum that explains the definition.